MUINJI'J

BECOMES A MAN

MUINJI'J

BECOMES A MAN

by
Saqamaw Mi'sel Joe

illustrated by Clara Dunn

BREAKWATER
100 Water Street
P.O. Box 2188
St. John's, NL
A1C 6E6

National Library of Canada Cataloguing in Publication

Joe, Saqamaw Mi'sel
        Muinji'j becomes a man / Saqamaw Mi'sel Joe;
illustrated by Clara Dunn.

ISBN 1-55081-167-3

1. Indians of North America--Juvenile fiction. I. Dunn, Clara
II. Title.

PS8569.O2652M83 2003   jC813'.6   C2003-900991-2   PZ7

The Canada Council | Le Conseil des Arts
for the Arts | du Canada

We acknowledge the financial support of The Canada Council for the Arts for
our publishing activities.

We acknowledge the financial support of the
Government of Canada through the Book Publishing
Industry Development Program (BPIDP) for our pub-
lishing activities.

Printed in Canada.

MICHAEL SHANNON JOE

January 29, 1972 - June 1980

To live in the hearts of those you love is not to die.

This book is dedicated to our son,

Michael Shannon Joe

who drowned in 1980 at the tender age of eight
and to all the little people in Conne River.

East

Muinji'j woke up to the sound of someone moving around. The first thing that came to his mind was 'Niskamij is up and getting ready to go on our trip and he's going to leave me.'

As he pushed back the warm qalipu skin blanket, he realized how cold it was and that it wasn't his niskamij he had heard. His dog, L'mu'j'i'j, had come into the wigwam during the night. He called L'mu'j'i'j and made the dog lie beside him. He snuggled down under his blanket again and became warm.

Muinji'j lay for the longest time looking up through the smoke hole. He could see the stars and count many of them. He imagined the trip he and his niskamij would take in the morning. They had talked about this trip for a long time.

Muinji'j realized that this was a turning point in his life. Once he made this trip with his niskamij to sell their furs at the big city, he would be a man. He would be selling his own furs. He would buy the things they needed for the coming winter. Muinji'j had already planned what he would buy for his nukumij. He would get her pretty fabric, needles and beads, and buy her a brand new, shiny skinning knife so she could help with the cleaning of the animals.

Muinji'j drifted off to sleep. He dreamed of the things he had thought about during his waking hours. He dreamed he was standing on the river-bank and his niskamij was leaving to go on a voyage to the big city without him. He was calling to his niskamij, 'Come back, Niskamij, and take me. I want to go with you. It's my turn.'

In his dream, the boys and girls in the village were laughing at him and calling him names because he cried. He loved his niskamij dearly and couldn't understand why he would leave him behind. He cried out again, 'Don't leave me, Niskamij. Don't leave me.'

Suddenly Muinji'j felt someone shaking him. It was his niskamij. "Get up boy, get up. It's time we start to get ready to go on our trip," he said.

Muinji'j then realized he had been dreaming. His niskamij had no intention of leaving him behind. He was actually going to the big city.

Muinji'j remembered the stories that had been told by people who had been to the city. They told of the fast pace, the big buildings and the delicious, sweet candy. Muinji'j planned on buying some of that wonderful candy with his money.

He jumped out of bed and greeted his nukumij. She said, "Go to the river and pay homage and give thanks to the spirits for all the good things we have. Wash your face in the clear, sparkling water. Face the East and thank the Kitpu for his protection. Face the South and thank the Nukumij. Face the West and thank the Spirit World for accepting you when it's your turn. Finally, face the North and thank the Great White Bear for all he has done for us. When you've done that, come back and I'll have breakfast waiting for you. Then we'll talk about your trip."

Muinji'j couldn't wait to get outside to do all the things he had to do. He was so anxious to be on his way that he rushed through some of the rituals he had done every day for most of his life. In his haste, he forgot an important thing he should have remembered. He forgot to thank the Nukumij.

Muinji'j came rushing back into the wigwam and sat beside his nukumij. She said, "Muinji'j, when you go on this trip to sell your furs, you will learn again all the many things we've taught you throughout your life about how to survive. You know there are fish in the rivers and there's food on the land. You know what berries to eat. You will be okay.

"You must remember the furs you're taking to the city are to buy things we need to get us through the winter moons. You have to be careful how you handle them and don't let them get wet.

"I want you to take care of your niskamij. He's getting old and fragile. He's not as strong as he used to be, so I want you to take care of him. Most importantly, if anything should happen to your niskamij, you have to look out for him. Make sure he's warm and comfortable.

"Remember, we will be praying for you and the spirits will be watching over you and your niskamij as you make this journey. Eat your breakfast while I prepare the bundle for you. I will put in your blanket and a good knife. I will also put in some of my favorite tobacco so that when the time comes to pray to the spirits for guidance, you can make your offering."

As Muinji'j ate his breakfast of lu'skinikn and qalipu meat, he could hear his niskamij moving around outside, preparing the canoe with the furs and other supplies they would take on their journey. Muinji'j almost choked on a piece of qalipu meat in his hurry to get outside. His nukumij looked at him and told him to slow down. She came over and handed him his bundle and said, "Remember, Muinji'j, we love you. You will have to be strong. You are the future leader of our people. Take care of your niskamij. I believe he is now ready to go."

Muinji'j hugged his nukumij before running out the wigwam door. When he got to the river, his niskamij was moving the canoe out into the water

with a smile on his face. Niskamij knew how important this trip was to Muinji'j.

Muinji'j sat at the front of the canoe and
Niskamij sat in the back. The canoe was heavily
laden with furs and supplies. Muinji'j felt good. The
sun shone warmly on his back. There was no wind
and the water was calm.

A crowd of young girls and boys had gathered to
see them off. They all waved goodbye. Muinji'j knew
the boys, who were younger than he was, were wish-
ing it was their turn. It made him feel proud and
privileged. It would be just his niskamij and him and
it would take many moons to reach the big city.

South

Muinji'j was anxious to be going. However, he knew his niskamij to be a very patient person and there would be no rushing.

Muinji'j paddled as hard as he could. Niskamij watched Muinji'j for a while before saying, "If you paddle too hard and too fast, you will quickly become exhausted. You need to pace yourself so you don't get tired. Or else you will be no help at all."

No matter how hard Muinji'j tried to be patient, he couldn't be. He wanted to see what was around the next bend. Meanwhile his niskamij sang softly to himself in Mi'qmac. Muinji'j could only think, 'I want to move faster. We've got so many things to see.' He was impatient and his niskamij's singing frustrated him.

They had paddled for some time when Niskamij said, "We have to go ashore now and make camp for the night. We will have pitewey and talk more about our trip to the city."

"But Niskamij, the sun is still high. Why do we have to stop? We'll never get to the city if we're going to stop every time you feel tired," said Muinji'j.

Niskamij laughed and said, "We need to stop because we have to make camp before dark. We can't wait until dark because then we'll stumble around and hurt ourselves. Then we'll never get to the city."

They found a nice beach. They had to take their canoe out of the water and unload their furs. After

they were done, Niskamij said, "Muinji'j, do you see that point of rock up ahead? Take your hook and line and go catch our supper."

Muinji'j's heart wasn't in what he was doing. As he walked he was talking to himself. He said, "The sun is high. I don't know why we have to stop when the city is so far away. Why do I have to go catch the old fish anyway?"

Muinji'j threw his hook into the water. Immediately, a great big trout hooked onto his line. All of a sudden he was excited. "Niskamij, Niskamij! Look, I've got a fish! I've got a fish!"

His niskamij looked over at him and smiled. He thought, 'If he's not careful, he's going to fall in and get wet. I'll have to dry him off and he's going to be mad.' Sure enough—SPLASH—Muinji'j fell into the water. He was swimming around and trying to hold onto his fish, but he couldn't do both. The fish got away.

Muinji'j came ashore all wet and cold and very disappointed. "Now I've ruined everything. I let our supper get away. We're going to be hungry tonight."

Niskamij felt sad for Muinji'j. "No, no, no, we're okay. It just shows that you have to be careful. You have to watch what you're doing and be patient," he said to Muinji'j. "I know how we could have something good for supper. My father taught me a good trick. We're going to make wood soup."

"Wood soup?" said Muinji'j. "How can you make soup from wood? That's not possible."

"Well, we'll see. You go back into the woods and find a nice stick that's not too dry and remove the bark from it," Niskamij said. "Bring it back and we'll make wood soup."

Muinji'j went into the woods. "My niskamij is crazy. He can't make soup from a stick. Maybe the cold air out here is doing something to him," grumbled Muinji'j. Suddenly he saw a nice stick. It looked like a bone from a bird's leg. "Perfect! If Niskamij can make soup from this, he's a real miracle worker," said Muinji'j.

Muinji'j took the stick back to the campsite. He was still all wet and soggy from his earlier swim with the trout. He walked with his eyes downcast, feeling sorry for himself.

Niskamij said, "You take off your clothes and hang them by the fire to dry. I'm going to make us some wood soup for supper." Niskamij dug out his old blackened pot to hang over the fire. He was singing and being cheerful.

Muinji'j took off his wet clothes. He was shivering from the cold when his niskamij came, wrapped him in a qalipu skin and sat him by the fire. He said, "You sit here and watch your clothes. Make sure they don't burn and I'll make supper."

Muinji'j mumbled, "Wood soup. I bet it is going to be really, really bad. Whoever heard of wood soup before?"

Niskamij smiled, went back to the pot and threw in the little stick. The only things in the pot were the hot water and the little stick floating at the top.

When the water boiled, Niskamij went to his bundle and when he came back he said, "Oh, look! I found a piece of qalipu meat. Maybe I'll add that to the pot." He went off into the woods and came back with an assortment of roots and plants. Soon the pot was full of different plants and wild vegetables.

Muinji'j thought to himself, 'This soup smells pretty good to be made from a stick.' He said, "Niskamij, are you pulling my leg? Are you really making wood soup?"

Niskamij said, "Come Muinji'j, see for yourself. See how good it looks."

The soup was delicious. Muinji'j ate and ate until he couldn't eat any more. He crawled into the lean-to with a big groan. The fire was burning outside and the stars were beginning to shine. Muinji'j was no longer in a bad mood. His niskamij sat by the fire and told him stories of his youth and of all the places he had been. Muinji'j slowly drifted off to sleep. That night, his dreams were of the big city, the fancy places his niskamij had talked about, the tall buildings and the people who were always in a hurry.

Muinji'j woke up to a new day. "Get up, Muinji'j," his niskamij said. "Get up. We have to move again. We can't stay here all day."

Muinji'j hurried to get up and put on his clothes and get ready for another long day. He went outside and found his moccasins, leggings and the jacket that had been dried by the fire. Niskamij said, "Don't forget to make your offering for the day, to give thanks for all the good things we have."

Off Muinji'j went to the river to make his offering. By this time, his stomach was growling. He was hungry and a little impatient to get on the way. When he returned to the fire, his niskamij had made pitewey and lu'skinikn, and warmed the wood soup from the night before. Muinji'j said, "I think I'll have more of that miracle soup, Niskamij." It was then that he realized his niskamij didn't look very well. He wondered what was wrong. "Are you okay, Niskamij?" he asked.

"Yes, Muinji'j, I'm fine. I'm just a little tired today. As soon as we eat, we'll load our canoe and head further along. We should reach the big river today if the wind doesn't blow and the spirits favour us. It's a mighty river, moving fast and furious. A lot of our people have lost their lives to that river. So, Muinji'j, today we have to be careful. Eat, my son, and when we're ready we will leave," said Niskamij.

Soon they had loaded the canoe and were paddling along the shore of the lake. A family of otters swam by. Muinji'j said excitedly, "Look, Niskamij. Look at the otters." A ti'am and her little

one were feeding along the river bank. Later that day, a qalipu swam across the lake in front of them. The wind was blowing softly in the trees. It was such a glorious day that Muinji'j wished it would last forever. At the same time he had never been this far before, and that made him excited, too.

Soon Muinji'j heard a noise that sounded like thunder. "Niskamij, is it going to rain? I hear thunder."

"No, Muinji'j, that's not thunder. That's the waterfalls near the beginning of the river. Do you see that mist ahead of us?" asked Niskamij. "That's the mist that rises from the waterfall. That's where we have to be careful, Muinji'j. We'll camp near the top of the waterfall tonight and tomorrow we'll portage around it."

Muinji'j didn't like the idea of stopping again. "How many more times do we have to camp before we get to the city?" he asked.

Niskamij said, "You have to have patience. It takes time to travel. We have to get all our furs down the river to the city. They can't get wet or all the work that we've done so far will be for nothing. and we won't have any supplies for the winter. We have to be careful. Maybe when we get to camp you can go catch a fish again, like the one you caught last night."

"Yeah, yeah, yeah," Muinji'j responded, "and maybe you can make more wood soup."

Niskamij laughed, "No, we'll have fish tonight. If you use patience and I lend you my hook and line, I am sure you can catch our supper."

On they paddled, hour after hour. Niskamij said, "We have to stop soon, Muinji'j, to have some pitewey and rest before we finish our journey for today."

They pulled into a sheltered cove with a white sandy beach and hauled in their canoe. They made a fire and soon the kettle was ready. Niskamij took out lu'skinikn left over from the morning and they had it for their lunch. They were soon on their way again.

After paddling for what seemed like forever, Muinji'j and his niskamij finally reached the start of the river with its roaring waterfalls. The mist hung over the river like a fog. There was a good landing place with a campsite they could use for the night.

The next day they would have to portage all their furs, supplies and their canoe around the falls before going further downriver to reach the ocean.

After making camp and cooking their supper, Muinji'j and his niskamij sat by the fire and talked about their journey the next day. Niskamij said to Muinji'j, "After tomorrow, you know, and another day's run, we'll be at the ocean. In one more day we'll get to the city. Are you excited, Muinji'j?"

Muinji'j tried not to show his excitement, but all

he could think of were the great sights he would see and the things he could buy with his own money. He hoped his niskamij could appreciate how he felt. He knew his niskamij, at one time, had been his age and must have gone through the same sort of excitement of making his first trip to the city.

After talking for many hours in front of the fire, his niskamij said, "It's time we slept, Muinji'j. Tomorrow we wake up early and make ready for our journey downriver."

That night they slept under the stars and listened to the roar of the river. If Muinji'j listened closely, he could hear the river talking. It spoke in a foreign language at times, but sometimes it sang the songs of his people and told the stories of ancient people who had come this way. Finally, Muinji'j slept and again dreamed of the city and all it had to offer.

Meanwhile, his niskamij lay awake and wondered if he was strong enough to move all their things around the falls and make the trip down the river. He had not told Muinji'j, but during the last day or so he had not been feeling well. He knew his strength was failing. He hoped, for the sake of Muinji'j, that he would be able to make this trip, but tonight he wasn't sure how he would do that.

In the morning when Muinji'j woke up, he wasn't sure what was happening. It looked like it would rain and the noise from the river was over-powering. He lay there and listened for a while until he realized it wasn't rain at all. The mist from the falls was making it look like rain. Suddenly he thought, 'Our furs will be ruined. They're all wet.' When he got up, he found that his niskamij had already taken care of the furs. He had somehow gotten up during the night and turned the canoe over. He had packed all the furs underneath the canoe so they would be safe and dry in the morning. Muinji'j wondered how his niskamij could be so strong and so thoughtful all the time.

After their breakfast of pitewey and lu'skinikn, Muinji'j and his niskamij started to portage their furs around the falls. Muinji'j wanted to show his niskamij how strong he was. He carried bigger loads and tried not to stumble. They made trip after trip. It was then that Muinji'j realized, 'If this is hard work right now, it is going to be even harder on the way back. We have to come back with all those supplies and do this over again.' But he felt that all the hard work was worth it. He was glad to be able to make the trip with his niskamij.

The last to be moved around the falls was the canoe. Muinji'j tried to help his niskamij as much as he could, but he wasn't tall enough to carry the canoe. He carried the bundles, the paddles and the remaining supplies. Along the trail his niskamij seemed to stumble. He also stopped many times. Muinji'j was worried that his niskamij was getting weaker.

When they had reached the river below the falls

and packed all their furs and supplies into the canoe, Niskamij said, "Muinji'j, I don't feel well. We may have to stay here for a while until I've rested."

Muinji'j was disappointed. He wanted to keep going, but when he looked at his niskamij, he could see the agony in his face and he felt ashamed. "Okay, Niskamij, we'll do as you say. Shall I make camp now and get firewood?" asked Muinji'j.

"No, Muinji'j, that's not necessary. We'll see how I feel as the day progresses and then we'll decide what to do."

He made a fire while his niskamij rested. He grabbed the fishing line and hook to catch a trout for dinner. He cooked the fish and made the pitewey. He was anxious to take care of his niskamij. Normally Niskamij had to encourage him to finish his chores, but today he needed no encouragement. His niskamij was sick and he wanted to keep him well.

After they had eaten, his niskamij lay back for a while and smoked his pipe. He said, "This is good. This is good because you are taking responsibility. You will be a man before you know it. Perhaps when you are a man, you will leave me behind and travel to the city to live."

"No," said Muinji'j. "I will be with you and my nukumij forever. That is my responsibility. That is my place."

Niskamij smiled and puffed on his pipe. He lay back and dozed for a while. After a short rest, they set off again.

As they travelled down the river that day, everything seemed quite normal. The sun was shining and eventually, the roar of the falls was left behind. Along the riverbank were places where tall grass grew. Every once in a while Muinji'j would see a ti'am or a qalipu, as well as flocks of ducks.

That evening the wind had changed and was blowing upriver. Muinji'j could smell something different. The air was fresh, clean and clear. The trees smelled fresh and the water tasted good. "Niskamij, what's that funny smell. It smells like something rotting," he said.

"What you smell is the salt sea air and when the salt air mixes with the fresh air it makes that smell," his niskamij explained. "Once you reach the sea, you will realize that it's not something rotting, but something very powerful. It's the sea that you smell. We're not far away now."

Just around the next bend in the river, Muinji'j saw the biggest lake he had ever seen in his life. He watched the huge waves that came up on the beach. He had never before seen the ocean and was greatly excited.

Muinji'j helped his niskamij pull the canoe onto the beach. He quickly knelt down to drink from this lake. Before his niskamij could say 'No, Muinji'j,' he had tasted his first salt water.

Instantly, he had to spit it out. He said, "Wow, this is crazy! This is so different, Niskamij. Is there something wrong with this water?"

His niskamij explained, "This is salt water. It is not fit for drinking, but there are things in this great lake, as you call it, like whales and seals. The salmon that we catch comes from this water. It tastes different from what you are used to, but it's alive. It was put here by the Creator. It just serves a different purpose. Tonight, we camp here and tomorrow we'll complete our journey to the city."

All night Muinji'j couldn't sleep. He tossed and turned, imagining what the journey would be like on the big lake. Every once in a while, he asked his niskamij, "Niskamij, how far is it to the city?"

"Oh, it's probably two days away. That is, if the wind is right and the waves are small because then we will make good time. If not, maybe we'll have to stay here for a month," his niskamij replied with a chuckle.

"A month! One whole month, Niskamij? How could we stay here for a month? We'll go crazy on this little beach with nothing to do. Nukumij will be worried and she'll send someone to look for us," said Muinji'j. He knew that his niskamij was just joking with him because he could see the smile on his face.

"No," he said. "It won't be a month, but it could be a couple of days."

Muinji'j finally fell asleep. When he woke up his niskamij was up, but Muinji'j knew immediately that he was sick. First Muinji'j felt disappointed, then concerned as he walked over to his niskamij.

Niskamij looked at Muinji'j and said, "I can't go anywhere today. I'm not feeling well. We'll have to stay here."

"Niskamij," said Muinji'j, "what can I do? How can I help you?"

"I don't know, Muinji'j. I don't know. It's my age and the hard work, you see. This may be my last trip to the city. The work is too much for me," Niskamij replied weakly.

Muinji'j gathered firewood and made a fire for his niskamij. He made pitewey, but his niskamij couldn't drink it. Finally, he said to his niskamij, "You lie down and rest."

All morning Muinji'j cared for his niskamij. "Niskamij, can I help you in any other way?" he asked. "Can I get medicines for you?"

"Yes, Muinji'j. Do you know the medicines I need?" Niskamij asked.

"I don't know, Niskamij, but if you can show me or tell me, I can gather them for you," said Muinji'j.

"First, Muinji'j, you have to climb to the flats above the river and find some beaver root. You reach into the water and pull out the roots from the pond. Then you must gather alder. After that, you will have to dig in the moss to find the yellow root. Next you must find and collect balsam fir and the leaves from the blueberry plant. Along the river you will find wild cherry and wild dogwood trees as well as ground juniper; collect some from these as well. If you can find those things and bring them to me, I will show you how to make the medicines to help me get well again," Niskamij explained to Muinji'j.

Although Muinji'j was worried about his niskamij, he was also proud and excited that his niskamij was trusting him with the sacred duty of collecting the medicines from the land. 'Maybe some day, I can be a medicine man,' Muinji'j thought to himself.

Off he ran to the top of the hill where he found a little pond. He quickly found the beaver root that his niskamij needed. As he looked around from the top of the hill, he could see way out and across the big lake. How glorious it looked. How strong and powerful, too. He wondered how they could ever cross it and reach the city.

Soon he was off again to find all the things that his niskamij had wanted. After many hours, he came back with all the plants and roots he had been instructed to find. He was tired, scratched and bruised, but feeling good to be able to help.

Niskamij asked Muinji'j to collect water from the river and make a fire. When the water boiled, his niskamij showed him how to prepare the medicines.

"Now," Niskamij said, "we need to build a sweat lodge. We have very little hide to make a covering, so this is what we'll do, Muinji'j. I want you to dig a hole in the sand as deep as you can make it for now. Then we'll make a fire. We'll put rocks on the fire to make them hot. We'll build a shelter over the hole using alders, birch bark, balsam fir boughs and anything else we can find. Inside, we'll put the hot rocks and we'll bring the medicine into the lodge. Those medicines that you have made will help make me well again."

Niskamij tried to help Muinji'j build the sweat lodge. When they had finished, it looked something like a beaver house. Muinji'j chuckled to himself. He'd seen sweat lodges before, but his looked different.

After Muinji'j had heated the rocks and put them in the lodge, he and his niskamij entered. Muinji'j poured some of the medicine onto the hot rocks to create steam. Niskamij drank some of the medicine. Muinji'j prayed with his niskamij to the Creator that all would be well again. He prayed for

his nukumij, he prayed for his people and he prayed for a safe journey. Above all, he prayed that his niskamij would remain strong for many years to come. He prayed that the medicine he had collected would make his niskamij well again so that they could continue with their journey.

After what seemed like many hours, they came out of the sweat lodge and his niskamij said, "I have to lie down now, Muinji'j, and let the medicine work. Tomorrow we will see what happens. So we rest now and wait until tomorrow to see what the Creator will have in store for us."

Muinji'j was so tired from the day's work that he fell asleep and, for the first time in many moons, he didn't dream. The next thing he knew, it was daylight; the morning had come and his niskamij was still lying down. That was strange. His niskamij had always been up in the morning.

Muinji'j was afraid that something had happened to his niskamij during the night. He inched a little closer and tried to listen. Slowly, he reached out his hand and touched his niskamij. "Niskamij," he said, "Niskamij! Are you okay?"

Slowly his niskamij opened his eyes and said, "Yes, Muinji'j, I'm still here, but I'm very sick and weak. I don't think I can make the journey to the city. I would like some pitewey. Will you make some for me? Then we will talk."

Muinji'j went outside, walked to the river and made a tobacco offering with the tobacco his nukumij had put in his bundle. He prayed to the East for protection for his niskamij. He prayed to the South to ask the Nukumij to come and protect his niskamij and make him well again. He prayed to the Spirits in the West that they would not take his niskamij yet. He prayed to the North, to the White Bear, to give him the strength, courage and wisdom that he needed to look after his niskamij.

When Muinji'j went back to their campground, he started a fire and made pitewey for his niskamij. He then sat and talked with his niskamij about the sickness that he had. His niskamij talked of the Spirit World and how important it was to be ready when the time comes for the spirits to take you and give you a seat of honour.

"Muinji'j, I'm old and I'm weak. I don't think I can make the trip to the city. If I taught you how to sail the canoe and if I taught you what to look for when you get there, would you be okay?" Niskamij asked.

"But, Niskamij, I've never been to the city before. I'd be too afraid," Muinji'j said.

"Come now, Muinji'j. There's nothing to be afraid of. Come and we'll go to the canoe and I will teach you how to sail the canoe by yourself," Niskamij urged.

Reluctantly, Muinji'j went, but his heart was sad. He loved his niskamij and he didn't want to leave him, but at the same time he was excited that his niskamij was trusting him and giving him so much responsibility.

Niskamij rigged the sail on the canoe and said, "Get in the canoe, Muinji'j, and try sailing around this little harbour. When you feel comfortable, we will load the canoe and you can sail to the city."

Muinji'j got into the canoe and sailed up and down the little harbour many times. His niskamij lay on the beach and watched him. Niskamij felt proud that Muinji'j was so strong. He had hoped, too, that Muinji'j would live with him and Nukumij forever. Niskamij knew the times were changing and soon Muinji'j would feel the draw of the outside world and would want to leave his home.

Finally, Muinji'j came ashore and said, "I'm ready, Niskamij. I'm ready to go to the city."

"Good," Niskamij said. "Let's load this canoe down with furs and we will see what happens. Muinji'j, I will stay here at the campsite and drink the medicines you have collected for me. I will try to get well so that when you return from the city, I will be strong enough to make the journey upriver with you.

"You go to the city and trade our furs. When you get the supplies, come back and meet me here. Beware, for there are many traps in the city. Muinji'j, you have to be tough. The trader will try to cheat you out of your furs. He will tell you that the furs are no good or that the prices he has to pay you are low. There are two traders in town. When you get to the trader, ask for the other trader, Pierre. Tell him you have furs to trade. Immediately the trader will know that he's got competition and he will want to give you a good price. So, as soon as you have the supplies, load them into the canoe and leave the city. Come back here and we will start our journey home. Muinji'j, be careful and extra cautious."

With that, Niskamij hugged Muinji'j. Muinji'j felt tears running down his face. He didn't want to leave his niskamij, but he didn't want his niskamij to see him cry so he turned his head and moved away. After a few minutes, he came back. "Okay, Niskamij, I'm ready to go."

West

Muinji'j got into the canoe loaded with furs and everything he owned, and sailed out through the little harbour. Before he rounded the point, he looked back and saw his niskamij standing there, holding his walking stick. He looked so frail. He waved to his niskamij and his niskamij waved back to him. Then he sailed around the point and his niskamij was lost from sight.

All day Muinji'j sailed along the coast line. He saw seals that day for the first time. They looked like big otters to him. He saw whales, too. He saw huge towering cliffs with waterfalls that came out over them. At times, Muinji'j was afraid and he wished that he could go back to be with his niskamij and feel the warmth and protection that he had always given to him. He knew he was on a journey to sell furs and get supplies, but he was also on a journey of strength and courage. He knew he must succeed, not only for his own sake but for the sake of his niskamij and his people.

It was nearly dark when Muinji'j decided he had to find a place to camp for the night. He knew he wouldn't reach the city that day.

After finding a nice beach and making sure his canoe and his furs were safe, Muinji'j was too tired to even make a fire. He curled up on the beach and fell asleep. That night his dreams were not of the city. He dreamed that his niskamij was well again and as strong and straight and powerful as he remembered him. He dreamed that his niskamij gave him directions on how to get to the city and what to do and what to say to make sure he made the best deal possible.

Muinji'j was awakened by a strange noise. Slowly he opened his eyes. On the beach all around him were seals. They were all over the place and Muinji'j was afraid to move. Finally, he stood up. His movement made the seals splash into the water. 'Wow,' he

thought, 'they're afraid of me. Now I don't have to
be afraid anymore. I'm the stronger one here.'

Muinji'j felt good. He made a fire and he made
some pitewey. He also had some of the lu'skinikn
that his niskamij had made. The morning was clear.
The sun was just coming up over the hills and the
strong, powerful smell of the ocean reminded him
of what his niskamij had said. The ocean was powerful and he had to be careful at all times. It would
decide whether you came or if you went. This
morning, the ocean was calm and Muinji'j said, "I
guess the ocean is saying that I can go now."

After he had finished his pitewey, he pushed
his canoe into the water and started paddling. He

paddled until just before dark. Ahead of him was a strange glow that looked like thunder and lightning had come down and stayed and Muinji'j was afraid. He wondered what it was. It was then that he remembered that his niskamij had talked about the strange light that they had in the city. 'This must be the city,' Muinji'j thought. There was no need to camp tonight. He would paddle until he reached the strange light.

Muinji'j paddled all throughout the evening and early night, trying to reach this red glow. As he got closer and closer, the light became more powerful. Muinji'j rounded the last point and what he saw in front of him looked unreal. The lights from the city made everything look different. There were strange smells blowing from the strange looking vehicles that were going back and forth. People were moving around, but no one spoke to each other. They all looked like they had somewhere they needed to get to fast.

Muinji'j slowly paddled closer until he found a place to land his canoe. It looked like a quiet spot where no one would bother him if he stayed for a while. It was too late to go and look for the trader.

Muinji'j sat on the beach for the rest of the night just looking in amazement at all the things that were happening. He said to himself, "Those people never sleep. They're moving around all night long. Don't they have any wigwam? Don't they have a nukumij to take care of them?"

Suddenly, Muinji'j felt lonely, longing for his own wigwam, his nukumij, and the people in his village. He went to sleep at a late hour. He wondered how his niskamij was doing. Was he okay? He was longing for all the things that were familiar.

Muinji'j knew that when dawn broke, he had to find a place to sell his furs so that he could return to his niskamij. Muinji'j drifted off to sleep.

When he woke up, the sun was high in the sky and people were moving again. Without even making pitewey, Muinji'j pushed his canoe out into the bay and went searching for a place to camp so he could get ready to do some trading. The day was bright and clear and Muinji'j was thankful.

As he paddled along the shoreline, people saw him and pointed at him as they talked to each other. Muinji'j couldn't hear what they were saying. Finally, he found a quiet cove. A house on top of a high hill overlooked the cove, but it was so far away that Muinji'j didn't think anyone would mind. He pulled his canoe into the cove before making pitewey and breakfast. While he drank his pitewey, he sat back and relaxed. Muinji'j again thought of his niskamij and wondered how he was doing. Muinji'j then fell asleep again and felt refreshed when he woke up.

Muinji'j knew that now was the time to go and see the trader. He realized, however, that he had no idea how he would get all the furs to the trader. He hoped that his furs would be safe while he was gone.

Muinji'j started up over the bank to the road that would take him into the city. As he walked along, he met people that pointed at him and wondered what he was doing. He was glad his niskamij had taught him the language of the city people, but everything else was unfamiliar. Muinji'j stared back at the people staring at him. 'Gee, they wear funny clothes,' he thought. Their shoes were shiny, their hair was short and they wore funny hats on their heads. The girls and the women wore long dresses

with big heels on their shoes. Muinji'j was amazed
how different the city people looked.

He found the store as his niskamij had
described. Muinji'j went through the doorway and
there were people all around. He was overwhelmed
by the sweet smell of candy. Immediately Muinji'j
knew this was the place where he would find his
candy and the sugar that his niskamij wanted.
Muinji'j was still a little afraid. As he stood there
looking around, the trader watched him and finally
he said, "What do you want, boy?"

Muinji'j said, "I have furs to sell, sir."

"You have furs to sell? What kind of furs do you have, boy? You have squirrels? You have rabbit furs?" he asked.

"No, sir," Muinji'j said. "I have beaver pelts, otter pelts, fox pelts, muskrat pelts and lynx pelts. I have all kinds of furs and they're good furs, too. My grandfather says they are good furs."

"Where is your grandfather, boy?" he asked.

"My grandfather is..." Muinji'j didn't want to tell him that his grandfather was so far away. "My grandfather is with the canoe, sir. He's watching the canoe. He asked me to come and see if you want to buy our furs."

"Well, I really don't want any furs. I have lots of furs and the prices are down," the trader said.

"That's okay," Muinji'j said. "My grandfather asked me to find out where the trader named Pierre is set up."

"Pierre! You don't want to talk to Pierre about furs; he'll cheat you, he'll rob you. Bring your furs here, boy. I'll give you a good deal even though I don't want any furs and the prices are down. Don't go to Pierre," the trader said.

"How would I get them here, sir?" Muinji'j asked.

"Well, I guess I could get someone with a horse and wagon to pick them up for you if you tell me where you are," the trader said.

Muinji'j answered, "I'm at the end of the road, in a big cove and there's a great big house on top of the hill nearby."

The trader responded, "Oh, good. I'll send a wagon there later to pick up your furs and talk with your grandfather."

"Okay," Muinji'j said, "I'll be there waiting."

Muinji'j turned to leave, but he was in such a hurry that he ran into someone. All he saw was white and fancy ribbons and long hair. Muinji'j fell down and knocked over a pile of apples. He scrambled to his feet and fell backward and landed in a puddle of water. He got up, embarrassed, as the trader came over to pick up his apples.

Muinji'j then noticed the little girl he had run into. She was standing there, mud splattered all over her pretty white dress. Her long hair was full of mud, but Muinji'j was stricken by her beautiful blue eyes. He had never seen eyes like that in his life. He tried to apologize, but all the girl could say was, "You! You! You! Do you see what you've done? You've ruined my dress!"

Muinji'j tried to apologize again. "I'm sorry. I didn't mean to."

Muinji'j stole one last look at those beautiful blue eyes and then he started to run. He didn't stop until he got back to the canoe. Finally, he sat down and he realized how funny the whole thing was and he laughed and he laughed until he cried. After a while he felt better and he wondered where the girl with the blue eyes had come from. 'Perhaps I'll see her again and perhaps this time she won't be so mad. Maybe she'll talk to me.' Then Muinji'j said, "Naa, that probably would never happen. Anyway, I have to get my furs ready."

He unloaded his canoe and unpacked all his furs. There were a lot of furs and Muinji'j counted how many pelts he had from the different animals. It was then that the horse and wagon the trader had sent to pick up his furs rounded the hill. The man only grunted when Muinji'j spoke to him. "Where's your grandfather?' he asked.

"He went into town. He left me here to load the furs. We'll meet him in town, sir." Muinji'j didn't feel good about lying, but if the trader knew he was alone, he would take advantage of it.

As he loaded the furs, Muinji'j looked up at the big house at the top of the hill and saw someone up there looking down at him. He asked the trader's helper, "Who is that?"

"Oh, you don't want to go up there, boy. Those people don't like you," the trader's helper replied.

"What do you mean, they don't like me?" Muinji'j asked in surprise.

"Well, they just don't like you, so don't go there. Don't bother them. Leave them alone," the trader's helper curtly replied.

Muinji'j hopped onto the wagon all loaded with furs and rode into the city to the trader's place. They started to haggle. Finally, Muinji'j got the prices his niskamij had said to ask for. Now, he hauled out the order that his nukumij had given him with all the supplies that she needed. At last, he had his own money that he could spend. He went around and picked out some beautiful fabric for his nukumij, some fancy thread and some new needles. He was very cautious about saving some money to buy his candy.

The candy jar was filled with Sugar Daddies. It was the same kind of candy that Muinji'j remembered. He could feel his jaw tighten. He knew how they were going to taste, how delicious they were. He bought enough candy, he figured, to feed the whole village for a month.

The trader sent the wagon back to the canoe with all the supplies and Muinji'j wondered how he would fit it all in the canoe. However, he knew this was the proper load and that it could be done. The trader's helper unloaded all the supplies and said, "I didn't see your grandfather."

"Oh, he's around. He's probably visiting his friends," Muinji'j said.

The trader's helper left and Muinji'j was standing there with all the supplies scattered all over the place. Right in the middle of all the supplies, he sat down and opened his first Sugar Daddy. Muinji'j felt like he was in heaven. The taste was unbelievable and he ate his fill before he went to sleep.

Just before dark he woke up. Standing there on the beach looking at him was the same girl he had splashed with mud and water earlier. She said, "What are you doing here?"

"I came for supplies," Muinji'j answered.

"Supplies for whom?" she wanted to know.

"These supplies belong to my grandfather," he answered.

"Where do you come from?" the girl asked.

"It's a long way away from here," he replied.

"But how did you get here? Who brought you here?" she continued.

"I brought myself," Muinji'j said. Suddenly he felt brave and he said, "Do you want a candy?"

"No, I don't want a candy," she said, "I'm not

allowed to eat those sugary things; they're not good for you."

"Oh, I think they're good," Muinji'j said. "I've never tasted anything like them in my life."

The girl came closer and said, "You smell funny."

He looked at her and walked around her before saying, "So do you."

She asked, "What do you mean, I smell funny?"

He said, "Well, you don't smell like the woods and you don't smell like you've got beaver pelt on you. You don't smell like the smoke and you don't

53

smell like the ocean. You have a different smell and that's funny."

The girl said, "You smell stinky."

Muinji'j said, "Well, so do you. You don't smell as good as me. I've got beaver pelt on me. I've got bear fat in my hair. I've got wood smoke all over me. I smell good. You smell funny. But I like your eyes. Your eyes are blue, just like the sky."

The girl's mood softened a little and she said, "You haven't told me what you're doing here."

"I told you I came to pick up supplies. These are my supplies for my grandfather and my grandmother," Muinji'j explained. "My grandfather is sick so I had to come here alone."

"How many days did it take you to get here?" she asked.

Muinji'j tried to figure out how many days the trip took and he said, "Well, I think it was about five moons to get here."

"That's a long time," she said.

"Oh, it was lots of fun with my grandfather. He is very smart and he knows all kinds of neat stuff. We live on the land and off the land," Muinji'j said.

"We live in that big house up on the hill," the girl said, "and we have servants to take care of us."

"What are servants?" Muinji'j asked.

"They're people who cook our food, clean our clothes, that kind of stuff," the girl answered.

"Oh, well, we don't have servants. All we have is my grandmother who takes care of us. I don't wash my clothes. I only have one set of clothes," Muinji'j said.

The girl said, "Yeah, I know. It smells like that too."

"You keep talking about my smell," Muinji'j said. "What's wrong with my smell?"

"Well, you smell funny. You smell different. Your hair is long. Has no one ever told you to cut your hair?" she asked.

"I can't cut my hair," Muinji'j said. "That would mean that I lose my strength. Then the spirits would stay away from me."

Muinji'j sat back and looked at the girl. He thought to himself, 'She reminds me of a little deer, the way she moves her head. Her eyes are so shiny and bright.'

The girl said, "I have to go. I have to go home."

Muinji'j said, "Maybe I'll see you next year?"

"Very unlikely," she replied. "Very unlikely." With that she turned and went back up the hill. Muinji'j watched her go, then turned back to his big load of supplies. He opened another Sugar Daddy and settled down for a long night.

North

In the morning, Muinji'j had been up for a while when the sun came up. He was all excited and had loaded his canoe and was ready to leave. He had to get back to his niskamij. He was so pleased with what he had done. He had made a good deal. He had gotten the supplies. He had been to the city.

Muinji'j didn't particularly care for the city and its funny smells, but he liked the girl. Maybe he would see her again.

Muinji'j pushed his canoe out into the bay and once he passed the city, he didn't look back. His only concern now was his niskamij and how he was feeling. Muinji'j paddled hard all day. Soon he would see his niskamij again. He rounded a point and pulled onto the sandy beach where he had stopped on his way up.

Muinji'j was so tired he couldn't unload his canoe. He lay on the beach and slept for a while. When he woke up, it was dark and Muinji'j knew he couldn't travel in the dark because it was too dangerous. He had to stay the night. He made a fire, some pitewey and something to eat and sat on the beach, looking into the fire for the rest of the night. He dreamed about the things he would do when he got home. He would be a hero. His people would be proud of him. His niskamij would be proud of him. 'I hope my niskamij is okay,' he thought to himself.

When daylight came, Muinji'j didn't waste any time. He pushed into the bay and started paddling. He paddled hard all day. He knew he was getting close to the mouth of the river. He knew he would see his niskamij soon. He was excited. His heart was beating faster and faster.

As Muinji'j rounded the point he saw the camp that he had left, but he couldn't see his niskamij. His heart was sad. 'Where are you Niskamij? Where are you?' he thought.

When Muinji'j got closer to the shore he saw his niskamij standing by the mouth of the river with a large fish in his hand and a smile on his face. He was okay. Muinji'j was relieved. He was so happy to see his niskamij.

His niskamij met him at the shore and held onto the canoe. He looked at the load of supplies Muinji'j had brought. "You did good. You did good, Muinji'j. Come ashore and have some fish. I've caught lots of fish. Your medicine was good. Your nukumij will be pleased we're okay."

With that, Muinji'j ran up to his niskamij and hugged him. For the longest time, they held each other tightly and both felt that everything in the world would be fine.

Glossary

Saqamaw	Chief
Muinji'j	Little Bear
Niskamij	Grandfather
Nukumij	Grandmother
Kitpu	Eagle
Qalipu	Caribou
Ti'am	Moose
L'mu'j'i'j	Little Dog
Pitewey	Tea
Lu'skinikn	Fried Bread

61

Acknowledgements

I would like to thank all of those who helped and encouraged me to write and publish this book.

May the Great Spirit grant you
the strength of Eagles Wings,
the faith and courage to soar to new heights,
and the wisdom of the ancients to carry you there.

Saqamaw Mi'sel Joe
March 2003

SAQAMAW MI'SEL JOE

Saqamaw Mi'sel Joe was born in Miawpukek on June 4, 1947 into a strong Mi'kmaq family; both his grandfather and uncle have held the office of hereditary Saqamaw. He has been educated in all the Mi'kmaq ways and traditions.

Currently, Mi'sel Joe is in his fourth consecutive two-year term as Administrative Chief. He is also the spiritual leader of his people. In this capacity he has gained recognition provincially, nationally and internationally, particularly in the area of spiritual healing.

Saqamaw Mi'sel Joe is committed to preserving the language, culture and traditions of his people. He plays a very public role in presenting a better understanding of the Mi'kmaq people of Miawpukek to residents of Newfoundland and Labrador and all of Canada.

He lives together with his wife Colletta and granddaughter Ansalewit at Miawpukek First Nation.